Word Wise with Wordsworth

raining cats and dogs—raining very heavily **(idiom, page 8)**

agitated—nervous or unable to relax **(adjective, page 10)**

alter—to make adjustments or changes **(verb, page 28, *altered*)**

awkward—uncomfortable or difficult **(adjective, page 7)**

capture—to catch and lock up a person or animal **(verb, page 19)**

collide—to bump into something or someone **(verb, page 27, *collided*)**

commotion—noisy confusion or activity **(noun, page 25)**

determined—strong-minded or firm **(adjective, page 10)**

eloquent—expressing a feeling or thought clearly
(adjective, page 14)

feat—a remarkable achievement **(noun, page 26)**

flimsy—weak and easily broken **(adjective, page 20)**

flinch—to make a small movement in response to something
surprising **(verb, page 12, *flinched*)**

index—an ordered list of items **(noun, page 29)**

might—power or strength **(noun, page 21)**

pounce—to make a sudden attack **(verb, page 16)**

rare—unusual or not often found **(adjective, page 14)**

rumble—a deep rolling sound **(noun, page 7)**

scruffy—messy or shabby in appearance **(adjective, page 13)**

squabble—a noisy argument over an unimportant matter
(noun, page 9)

submerged—completely underwater or flooded **(adjective, page 18)**

valiant—brave and heroic **(adjective, page 23)**

Cover design by Mark A. Neston Design

SCHOLASTIC, Word Advantage, Time Files, and associated logos are trademarks and/or registered trademarks of Scholastic Inc.

Published by Scholastic Inc., 90 Old Sherman Turnpike, Danbury, CT 06816.

For information regarding permission, please contact the publisher.

ISBN 0-7172-8690-8

Printed in the U.S.A.

First Printing, February 2007

TIME FLIES™ Book 7

Raining Cats and Dogs

by Quinn Alexander
Illustrated by Kelly Kennedy

SCHOLASTIC INC.

New York Toronto London Auckland Sydney
Mexico City New Delhi Hong Kong Buenos Aires

The Cloverhill map was lost! Marco blamed Abby for losing it, but she was sure it was Marco's fault.

"We've always kept it in your desk," Abby said. "If it isn't there, where did you put it?"

"I didn't put it anywhere," said Marco. "*You* had it last. Where did *you* put it?"

The kids had found the map the day they had started their after-school project on the history of their town. The map was nearly blank at first. But each time they returned from an adventure back in time—led by Wordsworth, the class pet—a new building or landmark would mysteriously appear on the map. To Abby and Marco, the changes on the map were proof that they had visited the Cloverhill of 100 years ago. But they were sure no one would believe them, so they hadn't told their teacher, Mrs. Harris—or anyone else—about their special map. That made it awkward to admit it was missing.

"I can't believe it," said Abby. "You're blaming *me* for losing the . . . um . . . special piece of paper?"

"That's right," said Marco. "It's your fault."

Just then a rumble of thunder rattled the classroom windows. It seemed that even the weather was angry today. Not long after lunchtime, dark thunderclouds had rolled in. Then once school was out, it had started pouring.

"It's **raining cats and dogs**, but that isn't the worst of it," said Mrs. Harris. "You two are *fighting* like cats and dogs."

"Well, Abby lost an extremely important part of our project," grumbled Marco.

"No I didn't! *He* lost—"

Mrs. Harris silenced them with a look. "If you two work together, you'll have a much better chance of finding whatever you lost," she said. "You certainly aren't getting anywhere with this arguing."

Another rumble of thunder filled the air.

Mrs. Harris suddenly opened her eyes very wide. "Oh, dear," she said. "I just remembered, I left the windows down in my car!" She grabbed her raincoat and headed for the door. "I'll be right back. In the meantime, I suggest you two end your squabble and join forces. *Teamwork* is the word!"

"*Teamwork* is the word! *Teamwork* is the word!" squawked Wordsworth.

The moment Mrs. Harris was gone, Wordsworth changed his tune. "Open the door! Open the door!" he sang out.

This was the signal that Wordsworth was ready to lead Abby and Marco back in time. But today, they weren't exactly in the mood to go on an adventure together. They glared at each other, still angry about the missing map.

Wordsworth was hopping from perch to perch, becoming more and more **agitated**.

"Well, I guess we had better let him out," Marco finally muttered. He opened the cage; and a moment later, Wordsworth flew out of the door and headed toward the custodian's room.

"Race you to Mr. Keys's room!" Abby shouted, dashing after the cockatoo.

"No fair! You got a head start," Marco yelled, angrier than ever.

The two of them took off. They were both so **determined** to win, they didn't even notice Mr. Keys, standing in the hallway.

"Marco! Abby! Wait," he called, trying to wave them down.

The kids didn't hear a word. They charged into the custodian's room at the same time, bumping into each other on their way to the supply shelves.

"I won!" Marco yelled.

"No way," said Abby.

While they argued, the rear wall of the room dissolved into a dark tunnel—their magic doorway back in time.

"Last one into the tunnel is a rotten egg!" Abby yelled, and they were off again.

There was a loud *pop*, like a *crack* of thunder, and a burst of bright light. The next moment they found themselves standing outside in the pouring rain. Their clothes had changed to old-fashioned outfits, a sure sign that they were in the Cloverhill of 100 years ago.

"It's raining cats and dogs in the past, too!" Marco shouted over the roar of the rain.

In a matter of seconds they were both soaked to the skin. They flinched as thunder cracked overhead. All thoughts of the map were suddenly washed away. Their anger was replaced by fear.

"Where are we?" Abby yelled.

"Look behind you! We're by the boathouse on the Big Muddy," Marco said.

Abby turned around. The river looked dark and dangerous in the downpour.

"Where's Wordsworth?" Marco asked.

Abby pushed a strand of sopping wet hair behind her ear. "I don't know, but I hear someone talking," she said. "It's coming from the boathouse."

The boathouse door was slightly open. Marco and Abby peeked inside—and they saw a large scruffy man. He was talking to someone out of view.

"Pretty birdie," the man said. "Polly want a cracker?"

"He must be talking to Wordsworth!" said Abby.

"Yeah, but where is he? I don't see him," said Marco.

"Polly want a cracker?" the man repeated, reaching out a hand.

"Crackers make me gag, and my name isn't Polly," came a voice from the corner. "Honestly, do I *look* like a Polly to you?"

Abby and Marco grinned. That was Wordsworth all right. He could only repeat words in the present, but he was quite eloquent when he visited the past.

The man staggered back two steps. "*You . . . you can talk!*"

"Of course I can talk," said Wordsworth, fluttering out of the shadows. "Now if you'll excuse me, I have to find my friends."

"Not so fast," said the man. "I bet someone would pay a lot of money for a rare bird like you." Without taking his eyes off of Wordsworth, the man started edging forward.

"That guy is trying to trap Wordsworth," Marco whispered.

"We'll have to stop him," Abby whispered back.

The man closed in on the cockatoo. "Can you do any other tricks?" he asked.

"I can sing and dance, but don't ask me to juggle. It's too hard on the wings," said Wordsworth, hopping sideways as the man tried to snatch him. "I can also do this!" He pecked the man's fingers and then fluttered his wings in the man's face.

"*Ow!*" the man bellowed, stumbling backward. He tripped on a pail and tumbled onto his back.

"This way, Wordsworth!" Abby yelled, throwing the boathouse door wide open.

"Sorry, I have to go. Time flies, you know," Wordsworth said. Moving as fast as lightning, he zoomed right over the man's head and out the door. Then he took off along the river's edge.

Marco and Abby ran after him, afraid that the scruffy man would **pounce** on them at any moment. Finally, Marco slowed down enough to look over his shoulder. There was no one in sight.

"Hold it, Abby!" he shouted, stopping to catch his breath. "The guy didn't follow us. In fact, I don't think he even saw us. He was only paying attention to Wordsworth."

Wordsworth landed on Abby's shoulder, and she burst out laughing. "Man, the look on his face when you started talking . . . ," she said.

"It *was* comical, wasn't it?" said Wordsworth.

"Yeah, it would have made a great picture," said Marco. "Hey! Do you think a digital camera would work, if we brought one with us to the past sometime?"

"Probably not," said Abby. "Our regular clothes don't even stay with us. So I don't think—"

"Help!" yelled a voice.

"Who's that?" Marco called. In the blinding rain, it was hard to tell where the shout had come from.

"It's me, Donald Ward. Help! I can't swim!"

Marco and Abby moved as close to the river as they could—without putting themselves in danger. But they still couldn't see who had called to them.

"Where are you?" Abby yelled.

"Over here!" came the voice from somewhere in the river.

"This way," Wordsworth called, taking off.

Marco and Abby followed Wordsworth along the riverbank. As they did, the man's voice became louder. "Help! Help!"

"There he is!" Marco shouted.

Donald Ward was near the middle of river. He was holding onto the branch of a **submerged** tree, as the fast-moving water tried to tear him loose.

"What should we do?" asked Abby. "There's gotta be some way we can help him."

"We need to find something he can grab onto," said Marco.

Wordsworth took charge. "Marco, I saw a coiled up rope in the boathouse," he said. "You go back there and get it. Abby, you go to the ferry dock to find help. I'll keep Mr. Ward company. Now go!"

The kids took off.

When Marco reached the boathouse, he found the door open—and no sign of the scruffy man who had tried to **capture** Wordsworth. Marco spotted the rope on the far wall, ran in, and grabbed it. Then he raced back up the path along the riverbank.

Marco couldn't see Wordsworth in the heavy rain, but he could hear the bird trying to keep Mr. Ward calm by talking to him.

"Help is on the way," Wordsworth called. "We're going to throw you a rope."

"Hurry!" shouted Mr. Ward. "This branch won't hold out too much longer."

The **flimsy** branch started to crack in the rushing water. But just as Marco was getting ready to throw the rope, the scruffy man came storming up.

"I'm looking for a big white bird. Have you seen one?" the scruffy man asked. Then he noticed the rope. "Hey, where did you get that? What do you think you're doing?" he demanded.

"I'm trying to save someone's life!" Marco shouted.

The man spotted Mr. Ward in the water. "What in the world?" the scruffy man gasped.

Marco hurled the rope as far as he could—but it came up short. Mr. Ward couldn't grab it without letting go of the branch.

"Here, let me give it a try," said the scruffy man. He snatched the rope from Marco's hands and coiled it up again. Then he flung it with all his **might**.

The rope landed close to Mr. Ward, who leaned forward, trying to grab it. For one terrifying moment he disappeared beneath the water. But he came up sputtering, with the rope in his hand.

Crack! The tree branch suddenly splintered and was whipped downstream by the foaming water. If Mr. Ward hadn't been holding onto the rope, he would have been swept away.

Just then Abby arrived with two other men—workers from the ferry dock. Everyone grabbed hold of the rope, and together, they pulled and pulled. They hauled Mr. Ward onto the bank, dripping and exhausted.

The men helped Mr. Ward to his feet, and everyone went to the boathouse. Only Marco and Abby noticed Wordsworth fly ahead and zip through the open door.

"Thank you, gentlemen," Mr. Ward said when he had caught his breath. Then his gaze fell on Marco and Abby, and his eyes brightened. "And thank *you*," he added with a smile. "Your **valiant** actions saved my life."

"You're welcome," said the kids.

Mr. Ward glanced around. "Is someone missing?" he asked. "I heard *three* voices when the children found me."

Just then the scruffy man spotted Wordsworth, who was perched on a crate, preening his feathers. "I bet it was that bird!" the man exclaimed. "It can talk as well as any human. I heard it." He stomped over and growled, "Say something, birdie."

Wordsworth cocked his head. Then he squawked, "Polly want a cracker? *Awk!* Polly want a cracker?"

The ferrymen burst out laughing, and Mr. Ward smiled. "I don't think I would call that talking like a human," he said.

"But it can say more than that—I'm sure of it," the scruffy man insisted, scratching his head. "It told me that crackers make it gag and that it can sing and dance."

The ferrymen laughed harder.

"*Awk!* Polly want a cracker?" Wordsworth repeated.

"The bird's name isn't even Polly," the scruffy man told the others. "Does it look like a Polly?"

Marco figured it was time to change the subject. He turned to Mr. Ward. "How did you end up in the river?" Marco asked.

"I'm a civil engineer, and I've been hired to study this stretch of the Big Muddy," replied Mr. Ward. "I was trying to figure out where it might flood its banks, and I got too close to the edge. I slipped on some rocks, and the next thing I knew, I was in the water. I'm sorry I caused such a commotion."

"That's OK. The important thing is that you're safe," said one of the ferrymen. "Now if you don't mind, we should be getting back to work. Looks like the rain is letting up."

As the men headed outside, Marco and Abby hurried over to collect Wordsworth.

"Congratulations! Saving Mr. Ward was quite a **feat**," Wordsworth said, hopping onto Abby's arm. "It seems that you two make a good team after all."

"That's right," Abby said with a smile. "*Teamwork* is the word."

"Open the door," said Wordsworth.

The kids spied a door at the back of the boathouse. They opened it, and with a *pop* and a *flash* of light, they were in the present. They had their own clothes on, and they were completely dry.

As Abby and Marco left the custodian's room, they nearly collided with Mr. Keys.

"I was trying to catch you on your way to my room," he said. "Did you two lose something?" With a grin, he held out the Cloverhill map.

Marco took it as if it were a precious gift. "Where did you find it?" he asked.

"In the garbage," Mr. Keys replied. "I found it when I emptied the trash can in your classroom. Someone must have accidentally thrown it out."

Marco and Abby exchanged sharp glances, each one tempted to blame the other. But then they both smiled.

"The important thing is that it's safe," said Marco.

"That's right," said Abby. "Thanks, Mr. Keys."

The kids rushed to their classroom and returned Wordsworth to his cage. Then they opened the map, to see how their latest adventure had **altered** it.

"Look!" Marco said, giving Abby a nudge. "The Roosevelt Bridge showed up. I wonder why."

"What's this about the Roosevelt Bridge?" asked Mrs. Harris, as she swept into the room.

"Oh, we were just . . . *uh* . . . wondering when the bridge was built," said Abby.

"I'm sure one of your history books would have that kind of information," said Mrs. Harris.

Abby got out *Cloverhill: 1900–1910* and looked up *Roosevelt Bridge* in the index. Then she turned to the page it listed and started reading. The book described how the bridge had been built over the Big Muddy in 1908 and named after Theodore Roosevelt, who was president at the time. When she reached the end of the page, it was her turn to nudge Marco.

"Guess what?" she said. "Donald Ward led the team that built the Roosevelt Bridge. That's the connection. That's why it showed up on the map."

"Cool," said Marco. "We helped save Donald Ward's life, and he helped build the bridge—and it's still there now."

"Good work!" squawked Wordsworth.

Get Your Word's Worth

After you finish reading this book together, use the prompts below to spark thoughtful conversation and lively interaction with your child.

♣ Marco and Abby were **determined** to help the man in trouble. Name something you feel determined about.

♣ Show me how you would get ready to **pounce** from behind a bush. Then do it.

♣ **Rare** items need special care. Tell me about something that you have seen that is rare. Why is it rare?

♣ A **squabble** is similar to an argument, but a squabble is about an unimportant matter. Let's make a list of five ways to avoid squabbles.